Hilary McKay

PRACTICALLY PERFECT

ILLUSTRATED BY HILDA OFFEN

Hodder
Children's
Books

A division of Hachette Children's Books

CONTENTS

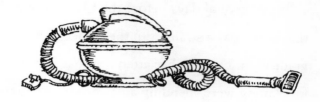

THE POET IN THE CUPBOARD

There was a poet living under the stairs at the palace. The Ladies-in-Waiting had put him there. They had pushed aside the palace clothes horse and mop bucket, draped a tablecloth over the vacuum cleaner, scattered around cushions and framed photographs of themselves and other poetical items, and then they had moved in the poet. They kept him there as a sort of pet, like an enormous, poetry-writing hamster. The poet had thick yellow hair and grass green eyes and he was very smiling and polite to the Ladies-in-Waiting.

The Ladies-in-Waiting thought he was perfectly wonderful.

It was several days before the Queen noticed that there was a stranger in the palace, but gradually it came to her attention that the Ladies-in-Waiting were spending an astonishing amount of time scurrying backwards and forwards to the cupboard under the stairs with supplies of net curtains and artificial flowers and fridge magnets and other such useful objects.

'It is so unusual to see the Ladies-in-Waiting looking busy,' she remarked to Michael the gardener's boy (and also the Queen's best friend). 'It's not like them at all. I'm sure they're up to something.'

'If you are worried you could ask the Cook,' suggested Michael. 'She will know what they're up to if anyone does.'

This was perfectly true. Of all the people who lived in the palace the Cook was the one who knew best what was going on. News seeped down into the kitchen like gravy into a tablecloth. The unnatural behaviour of the Ladies-in-Waiting had seeped down with the rest and the Cook was only too happy to explain it to the Queen and Michael.

'Ah!' she said, sighing romantically and wiping jam off her chin. 'It's love, that's what it is! They've got a poet in that there cupboard, and whatever he fancies is his for the asking because they're every one of them swept off their feet with emotion!'

'Oh!' she continued, ignoring the Queen and Michael's astonished faces. 'You may stare but sooner or later we are all caught out! It was the Butcher for me but that is all in the past. There is no need to stand there with your mouths hanging open. He is a fine young man and partial to cheese and beetroot sandwiches and cold kidney pudding which I send in every night because true love must have its way!'

'Cold kidney pudding?' asked Michael in horror.

'Boiled in a bag,' said the Cook. 'The Butcher was the same and yet it was over offal that I lost him. Still, better to have loved and lost …'

'She's gone mad,' said the Queen, watching dispassionately while the Cook cheered herself up with another spoonful of jam. 'Mad, and it sounds like the Ladies-in-Waiting have as well. Let's go and look at that poet.'

'Well, there's definitely something wrong with him,' said Michael, as he followed the Queen out of the kitchen and up staircases and down passages. 'Definitely, or else he wouldn't.'

'Wouldn't what?' asked the Queen, pausing at the door of the cupboard under the stairs.

'Cold kidney pudding,' explained Michael.

'Oh, yes please!' exclaimed a voice from within, and the Queen pulled open the door and there was the Poet, sitting on the vacuum cleaner and eating cold baked beans out of a saucepan.

'More pudding?' he asked.

'Certainly not!' said the Queen.

There were a few moments of silence while they glared at each other.

'Do you know who I am?' asked the Poet sternly.

'You're a Commoner,' said the Queen.

'A Commoner!' repeated the Poet indignantly. 'I'm a Poet!'

'I'm a Queen,' said the Queen briefly, and the Poet went suddenly pale.

'Excuse me. I must think,' he said shakily and shut the cupboard door.

'That surprised him!' remarked Michael.

'I don't know why,' replied the Queen. 'Do I look like a Lady-in-Waiting?'

'Not a bit,' said Michael, 'but neither does he look like a poet, poor beast!'

'Why poor beast?' asked the Queen.

'Cold kidney pudding,' explained Michael patiently, and at that moment the door was pushed open again.

'Oh Hail Your Majesty!' proclaimed the Poet bowing deeply with the bean saucepan in one hand and a piece of paper in the other. 'Hail Your Majesty!'

'You've said that,' interrupted the Queen.

'Ha …' began the Poet again. 'I mean to say …'

'What?' asked the Queen.

'Well what about having a Poet?' asked the Poet. 'Every home should have one you know. Every palace I mean. Think of the convenience! Instant poems for all occasions! Elegant, reliable, economical and always to hand! No undertaking too small ...'

'I should think not,' said the Queen severely.

'All I ask,' said the Poet, 'is shelter under your roof ...'

'Stairs,' interrupted the Queen.

'Stairs,' agreed the Poet meekly, 'and the odd slice of pudding.'

('Poor beast,' said Michael.)

'Yes, but can you write poems?' asked the Queen.

'Oh yes,' said the Poet eagerly, 'and the Ladies-in-Waiting are very fond of me!'

'Don't snigger!' said the Queen.

'Oh, all right,' said the Poet, 'but I think you ought to know that Poets in other palaces are

treated with great respect and called the Poet
Laureate and given quite a lot of money.'

'Not in this palace though,' said the Queen
firmly. 'But you can write me a poem and I will see
what I think. Write it,' she added as she shut the
cupboard door, 'about the Royal Donkey. That is a
nice easy thing for you to start on and I will come
back to listen to it later.'

For a long time there was silence in the cupboard
under the stairs, and then muttering.

'Donkey,' heard the Ladies-in-Waiting as they
listened at the keyhole. 'Donkey. Conkey. Gonkey.
Honkey. Plonkey. Wonkey.'

'He is composing,' they whispered to each
other, and instead of knocking they left their
offerings of lampshades and hairslides and padded
photograph albums in a respectful heap outside
the cupboard door. The Poet fell over them when
he came out to recite to the Queen.

'These ridiculous old ladies!' he exclaimed
irritably, kicking at the lampshade which had
jammed on to his foot. 'They are forever appearing
with useless ...'

'Poem,' said the Queen.

'Oh yes,' said the Poet (getting up from the
photograph albums and removing a couple of
hairslides that had been stabbing him through his
trousers). 'Poem,' and he recited,

'Twinkle twinkle, Gonkey Donkey,

How I wonder if you're Conkey

Up above the world so high

Like a diamond in the sky

Twinkle twinkle Honkey Plonkey

Hope your legs are not too Wonkey!'

'Horrible,' said the Queen. 'No pudding for you tonight.'

'No pudding?' asked the Poet.

'And I'm sure I've heard something almost exactly like it before,' added the Queen.

The Poet burst into tears and said that was a terrible thing to say to a poet, and that it wasn't fair and nothing rhymed with donkey, and then he stamped back into the cupboard and kicked the vacuum cleaner.

'That is his artistic temperament,' sighed the Ladies-in-Waiting and they said it was only to be expected and then they began to quarrel about who had been so silly as to leave lampshades and photograph albums and hairslides right where he could fall over them, and to argue about which of them the poet liked best. The Queen left them to it and went off to compose a poem about the Royal Donkey to prove it was possible and in a matter of seconds she found that it was, and in a matter of minutes it was written.

Little Donkey,
Silver-grey
Sweet as clover
Soft as hay.

'Poetry writing is easy!' she told Michael triumphantly, but the Poet Laureate did not appear to find this to be so, and it seemed to the Queen that the more he wrote the worse it became.

'It's the Treasurer's birthday soon,' she told him the day after she had shown him her donkey poetry. 'I shall need a special poem to recite at his party.'

Sing a song of sixpence, wrote the Poet,
A pocket full of rye
Happy Birthday Treasurer
Baked in a pie.

Only the Ladies-in-Waiting admired that poem. The Treasurer simply hated the idea of being baked in a pie and the Queen remarked once again that it reminded her very strongly of something she had heard in the past. In the end she had to write the Treasurer's birthday poem herself.

The Treasurer is eight-five
Thank goodness he is still alive
If he were not he would be dead
And who would do the sums instead?

This was much more the Treasurer's idea of poetry, accurate and to the point and making him feel needed. When it was read aloud at the birthday party the Poet stomped off to the cupboard and sulked for a week and refused to even consider the Queen's suggestion that he should write a humorous poem about the Cook. So the Queen wrote one instead. It was:

The Cook
Cooks muck.

She thought it was extremely funny and so did Michael.

Meanwhile the Ladies-in-Waiting were becoming a terrible nuisance. Each of them declared that she was the only one who truly understood the Poet, and they filled the palace with their quarrels about who was the fattest or thinnest or prettiest or most poetical. Also, piles of impractical offerings (which the Poet rudely called junk) began to block the corridor outside the cupboard under the stairs, the Cook got tired of making kidney puddings, and the Queen got even more tired of smelling them cooking.

'This poet,' she said to Michael one day, 'is more trouble than he is worth! And look at the poem he wrote about me this morning!'

'Send her victorious,' read Michael,
'Happy and Glorious

Long to reign over us ...'

'I'm perfectly sure I've heard it before,' said the Queen. 'Something must be done and I shall do it today because what with the pudding fumes and the Ladies-in-Waiting this palace is becoming impossible to live in.'

Michael said she was quite right, and that evening when the Ladies-in-Waiting were all in the garden weaving flowers into their hair she went to the cupboard under the stairs and told the Poet Laureate that she could stick it no longer.

'It is not your awful poetry that I mind so much,' she explained, 'because I have discovered I can write all the poetry I need as easy as pie and it is much better than yours. But the smell of those puddings is too much ...'

'I could give up the puddings,' interrupted the Poet.

'And the Ladies-in-Waiting have become quite

unbearable since they fell in love with you. If you want to stay here you must choose the one you like best and put the rest out of their misery.'

'And what am I supposed to do with her when I've chosen her?' demanded the Poet sulkily.

'Marry her of course,' said the Queen.

'Marry her!' shouted the Poet. 'What me? Me marry one of those awful Ladies-in-Waiting? Me? The Palace Poet Laureate! Never! Never! Never! Never! Never!'

'I've heard that before as well,' said the Queen.

But the poet was past caring about plagiarization. His only concern was that he should not be forced to marry a Lady-in-Waiting and he begged the Queen to help him avoid this terrible fate.

'I shall have to flee the country,' he said packing pieces of pudding in pieces of paper as he spoke, 'flee the country and never come back. They are all of them terribly plain.'

'I am afraid they will flee after you,' said the Queen. 'The Ladies-in-Waiting are excellent runners considering their age.'

The Poet Laureate became even more distressed at this news and he said in his despair that the Queen might help a fellow poet and added (peevishly) that they could not all be Queens.

'No, nor Poets either,' remarked the Queen, but all the same she was sorry for the Poet. He was, as Michael often remarked, a poor beast and she thought of a plan to help him.

The next day a notice appeared on the door of the cupboard under the stairs. It was entitled CARE OF YOUR POET and it read,

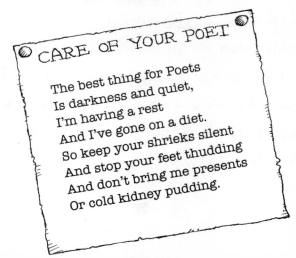

CARE OF YOUR POET

The best thing for Poets
Is darkness and quiet,
I'm having a rest
And I've gone on a diet.
So keep your shrieks silent
And stop your feet thudding
And don't bring me presents
Or cold kidney pudding.

The palace was much more peaceful that day. The Ladies-in-Waiting quarrelled in whispers in the garden instead of in screeches in the palace. No kidney pudding was cooked and no presents left outside the Poet's door, although the Ladies-in-Waiting could not resist scattering little bunches of flowers for him to find when he emerged.

But it seemed that the Poet did not even want flowers. The poem that was pinned to the door the next day was ungratefully blunt.

> The view from my keyhole
> Grows horrid and horrider
> Sweep up that rubbish
> And tidy the corridor.

The Ladies-in-Waiting did as they were told but not very gracefully.

'He has grown so cold and distant,' they complained to the Cook.

'That is men for you,' agreed the Cook. 'Blow hot, blow cold. If it's not offal it's insolence! He's been told by the Queen he must take his choice and make an honest woman of one of you and in my opinion the thought is too much. He's been off his pudding these past two days, and it's only to be expected!'

That night the Ladies-in-Waiting could not sleep for wondering if the Cook was right, and if she was, which one of them was about to be made an honest woman of by the Poet with the grass green eyes. They leapt out of bed the next morning in their eagerness to reach the cupboard under the stairs in case there should be a new poem. And there was a new poem. And the Ladies-in-Waiting read it with fury and disbelief and then they ripped it off the door and tore it in to little pieces and went to search for the Poet. But the cupboard was empty and the dust on the vacuum cleaner showed that it had not been kicked for several days. It was perfectly plain that the Poet had fled.

'Whatever is the matter?' asked the Queen, coming to see how they were getting on, and the Ladies-in-Waiting said nothing was the matter and when she asked how the Poet was they replied, 'What Poet?'

So the Queen knew that her plan had worked and the Poet had escaped with at least forty-eight hours start on the Ladies-in-Waiting and the Ladies-in-Waiting were no longer in love. The last poem on the cupboard door had been too much for them. And when she showed Michael the secret copy she had kept for herself he said he was not surprised.

Oh Ladies-in-Waiting, it's come to the crunch
I've been told I must marry
the pick of the bunch
This means I must cancel the future I'd planned
For some things are more than a Poet can stand.

When I came to this palace my only thought was
To do for my living as little as poss
To compose Royal Rhymes is enough of a task
And coupled with marriage is too much to ask.

And so I have fled to a far distant city
Where the Poets are free
and the ladies are pretty
Farewell and goodbye! It is time to explain
You Ladies-in-Waiting are waiting in vain!

'I think it's my best,' said the Queen.

A NIGHT IN THE STABLES AND A DAY AT THE RACES

'I'm bored,' said the Queen, 'I'm bored, I'm bored.
What can I do? Can I teach the Prime Minister to
play Snap?'

'No,' said the Prime Minister's wife. 'Leave him
alone. He has settled down now.'

'Well, shall I tidy out the Diplomatic Bag?'

'No, thank you.'

'Tell you what I want for Christmas?'

'No, thank you.'

'What about setting off the fire alarm to

surprise the Ladies-in-Waiting?'

'I don't think that would be a good idea,' said the Prime Minister's wife firmly.

'Do you think we might make the Cook marry the Butcher and let me be Bridesmaid?'

'It wouldn't be very kind to the Butcher would it?' said the Prime Minister's wife.

'What do you suppose the Treasurer wears under his ki—'

'Really!' exclaimed the Prime Minister's wife. 'It has never crossed my mind to wonder! What you need is a nice quiet hobby! Something to keep you occupied!'

And everyone in the palace said she was quite right and the Cook suggested Bingo and the Treasurer suggested Higher Mathematics and the Prime Minister's wife suggested Hockey and the Ladies-in-Waiting said what about tidying her bedroom for a change. The Prime Minister did not suggest anything but he agreed with the rest, and then Michael wandered in and suggested Horse Racing.

Everybody groaned because of all the expensive and inconvenient hobbies the Queen might have chosen, Horse Racing was by far the most expensive and inconvenient, and it was just like Michael to have suggested it.

'You encourage her!' said the Prime Minister's wife crossly. 'Hockey would have been perfectly adequate!'

'I should have needed twenty one other Queens to play with,' pointed out the Queen. 'And a hockey stick! Horse Racing is perfect and I already have the Royal Donkey. All I shall need is a racetrack.'

After that there was no talking her out of it. Pointing out the enormous cost of racetracks and the obvious inability of the Royal Donkey to compete against racehorses was useless. The Royal Donkey gallantly agreed to race (although he did

not guarantee to win), and Michael remarked that
the cost of the racetrack could easily be covered
by a tiny, hardly noticeable, rise in taxes.

('Not again!' groaned the Treasurer.)

'It would be different if that donkey had the
slightest chance of winning,' said the Prime
Minister's wife.

'He might,' said Michael.

'And even if he doesn't,' said the Queen, kissing
the Royal Donkey, 'nobody will be cross.'

'Of course not,' agreed Michael.

'But wouldn't it be lovely if he did,' said the Queen.

'Perhaps he will,' said Michael.

And so the racetrack was built, and miles of white fences erected, not to mention stables for visiting racehorses, a large band stand, and several small tables with umbrellas over the top.

'I suppose you will be riding the Royal Donkey yourself,' said Michael, and the Queen said of course she would. She had already chosen her racing colours, gold and silver, gold for the Queen and silver for the donkey, with small silver horse shoes embroidered on the gold, and small golden crowns embroidered on the silver.

'Completely unnecessary,' said the Prime Minister's wife.

'Beautiful,' said Michael.

When everything was ready invitations were sent out, and because it was considered a great honour to be asked they were all accepted with

thanks, and one exciting afternoon all the visiting race horses who were to run the next day arrived. There were nineteen of them so that the Royal Horse Race should be twenty horses wide (or nineteen and one donkey to be perfectly exact). The visiting jockeys arrived too, and they were very surprised when they heard that the Queen would be riding against them. They looked at her silver and gold colours (which she was already wearing because she could not bear to take them off) and they grinned at each other.

'Your first race too!' they said to the Queen.
'Fancy that! Are you nervous? Aren't you scared?
Well I never!'

Until that moment the Queen had not been
scared, but by the time the nineteenth jockey had
grinned his grin and remarked that she must be
terrified she was beginning to think that they
might be right. Michael saw how she was feeling
and took the jockeys away to see the sights of the
town, and the Queen went to bed because she
could think of nothing else to do. And she lay
awake in the dark and wondered for the first time
exactly what it would be like riding the Royal
Donkey against the nineteen fastest racehorses
in the kingdom. Would they jostle very hard at the
bends, she wondered, and what if they bumped
the Royal Donkey and what if she fell off and
the nineteen racehorses didn't see her on the
ground and raced over her with their seventy-six
hard hoofs?

'It would be sure to ruin my beautiful gold and silver,' thought the Queen miserably. 'I wonder how big those racehorses actually are!'

This last wonder was the most bothering of all, and when it had bothered the Queen for several hours she could bear it no longer and she got out of bed and tiptoed down to the Royal Stable to see for herself, and there she had a terrible shock.

In the twentieth stable the Royal Donkey slept peacefully on his pillows, but in the other

nineteen stables there was no sleep. Nineteen
enormous heads hung gloomily over their stable
doors. They were roughly twice as high up as the
Queen had expected to find them, but it was not
this that startled her so much. She had never seen
a racehorse close up before and she was not at all
prepared for the shape of them. There was none of
the Royal Donkey's comfortable roly polyness
about them at all. Their huge dark eyes gazed
mournfully at the moonlit Queen and all of a

sudden she stopped being afraid and began to be very cross instead. She opened the stable doors and looked carefully at those racehorses and it was as she had suspected.

'Starved!' said the Queen, and she remembered the days when she had first owned her Royal Donkey, and how unwell he had become through her not knowing what to feed him, and now here was the same problem all over again, only nineteen times worse. The racehorses had legs no fatter than the Royal Donkey's, although at least two or three times longer. Their fur was so smooth and flat that in places it was possible to see their ribs and, compared to the Royal Donkey's, their stomachs were practically invisible.

'Don't worry,' said the Queen. 'I know exactly what you need, and there is plenty of everything because of the Royal Donkey.'

Then for the rest of the night the Queen feasted those racehorses. They ate oats and carrots

and apples and donkey nuts and armloads of hay
and bran-with-molasses-and-raw-eggs and sugar
lumps and fresh clover gathered by moonlight
from the Royal Paddock. They ate all night. It was

not until dawn that their heads began to nod and their eyes to close, and then they nuzzled the tired Queen lovingly, and curled up on their straw and went to sleep.

Feeling very noble and contented the Queen went back to bed and fell so soundly asleep that it was quite late morning when she woke. Downstairs the palace was full of noise and confusion and the Queen could not help noticing that everywhere she went she bumped into jockeys staggering around drinking orange juice and holding their heads and groaning. Obviously Michael had shown them the sights most thoroughly the night before.

'Cor that Michael,' she heard one of them say as he walked into a wall. 'He's a lad! Where's my whip?'

'Where's your what?' asked the Queen (who had woken up feeling as bright as sunshine and as fresh as a rose).

'Whip,' repeated the jockey groping round with his eyes shut because the light was so dazzling. 'Small stick carried in the hand for the hittin' of the hoss.'

'Nobody's hittin' hosses on my racecourse,' said the Queen, and the jockey said she must be joking and the Queen assured him that she was not. Then all the other jockeys crowded round and demanded to know how they were supposed to make their horses run without whips.

'Talk nicely to them,' said the Queen airily, 'like I do to the Royal Donkey,' and she hurried outside before the jockeys could argue any more.

Already people were beginning to gather along the white painted rails, and at the umbrella-covered tables little men in hats were taking money from passers-by. Michael was talking earnestly to one of them who sat beside a blackboard on which was chalked the words,

Michael explained that this meant that the little man thought the Royal Donkey's chances of winning were one in a thousand, and he added that all the other little umbrella men were of similar opinion.

'What cheek!' exclaimed the Queen.

'And,' continued Michael, 'that means if you give them, say, tuppence and the Royal Donkey wins then they have to give you a thousand tuppences back. But if the Royal Donkey should happen to lose then he keeps it.'

'The Royal Donkey?' asked the Queen alarmed.

'No, the tuppence,' said Michael. 'That is their way of getting rich.'

'It sounds a very slow way,' said the Queen.

'I know,' agreed Michael, 'but as a matter of fact they are all millionaires, those little men. I don't suppose you've got tuppence you don't want on you have you?'

The Queen obligingly turned out her pockets but found nothing but a few handfuls of gold coins.

'Sorry,' she said to Michael, but Michael said that it would do just as well and when the Queen looked round a moment later he was talking to the little umbrella man again.

'He's trying to get him to change his mind,' thought the Queen and then she arrived at the stables and forgot about everything in the hurry of preparing breakfast for nineteen racehorses and one donkey. Already it was wonderful to see how much the racehorses had improved. Midnight feasts and breakfast in bed suited them exactly. Their ears were pricked and their appetites were wonderful and already their stomachs were nearly as large as the Royal Donkey's. It was plain to see that all nineteen of them were head over heels in love with the Queen. They watched her, bright-eyed, wherever she went.

Breakfast was over and the horses were just beginning to wonder if there was time for a sleep before lunch when the jockeys arrived. None of the racehorses felt at all like running and they were most unhelpful about standing up and having their saddles put on. While the jockeys were busy with their horses the Queen had a private word with the Royal Donkey.

'Do not run too fast,' she whispered. 'I am afraid those racehorses are not as strong as I thought they would be and it would be a shame to beat them by too much. And besides, it would make the jockeys cross.'

The jockeys were cross already. They had woken up with terrible headaches (thanks to Michael) and had had their whips taken away from them (thanks to the Queen), and now, for some mysterious reason the horses' saddles appeared to have shrunk in the night. No amount of tugging at the straps would make them fasten round the horses' middles and in the end the jockeys had to settle for balancing them on top.

'It's going to be jolly wobbly when they get

going really fast,' remarked the Queen to the Royal Donkey, and the racehorses seemed to realise this and walked very slowly and carefully up to the starting line of the Royal Race Course. And when they were all lined up with the Queen in the middle (because she was Queen) the Prime Minister climbed up on to a small table and shouted, 'One to get ready!'

There was a murmur of excitement from the crowds gathered along the white rails. The racehorses yawned sleepily.

'Two to get steady!' continued the Prime Minister, consulting a piece of paper.

The nineteen racehorses looked at him as if he was mad, dropped their heads, and began to eat grass.

'Starved!' said the Queen.

'Three to GO!' shouted the Prime Minister, and fell off the table.

Only the Royal Donkey started at once. For a

moment it seemed as if the jockeys might have to get off and push. Luckily the Queen, glancing back over her shoulder to see how much she was winning by, noticed what was happening (or not happening).

'Follow me!' shouted the Queen.

So then the racehorses (who knew a Royal Command when they heard one) picked up their feet and started to trot, the jockeys sighed with relief and the little men under the umbrellas (who had gone very silent and thoughtful) began to sit up and take hope. But the crowd groaned with disappointment because they would have liked to have seen the Queen and the Royal Donkey win and the racehorses were catching up with them very quickly.

'Come on Your Majesty!' they shouted. 'Go! Go! Go!' And the little donkey heard them and went faster than he had ever done in his life, but the racehorses grew closer and closer until they were

almost treading on his heels. And then the jockeys
wished they had their whips. Because no matter
how nicely they talked to their racehorses they
could not seem to go past the Queen. And the
finishing line grew closer and closer and the
crowd roared louder and louder and the men

under the umbrellas grew paler and paler and the
Prime Minister climbed back on to his table and
said, 'Why are they all coming back?'

But nobody noticed him. The crowd was too
busy cheering and the Queen was too busy riding
and the racehorses and the Royal Donkey were

too busy running and the jockeys were leaning over to their horses' ears and demanding with desperate earnestness that they overtake the Queen immediately.

But it was already too late. The donkey gave an extra large bounce, there was a flash of light across the finishing line like a gold and silver comet, and the roar of the crowd was like a gale in the forest because the Queen had won.

That night when the crowds had gone home and the little donkey had been put to bed and the Queen was admiring the golden cup that she had awarded herself, Michael arrived at the palace pushing a very heavy wheelbarrow.

'It's your winnings,' he told the Queen. 'It should easily be enough to pay for the racecourse. I got it from the money you gave me for the umbrella men.'

'Didn't they mind?' asked the Queen astonished, and Michael said that they had minded very much at the time but they were already beginning to recover. And they had said tomorrow is another day and had paid up handsomely.

'Now tell me how you did it,' said Michael.

'Did what?' asked the Queen. 'Wasn't the donkey brilliant?'

'Brilliant,' agreed Michael, 'but how did you make the racehorses run like that? Almost catching you up but never quite doing it? It was fantastic!'

'It was easy,' said the Queen after some thought. 'I just said "Follow me". And they did.'

'I should never have thought of that,' said Michael.

'You probably would have,' replied the Queen sleepily. 'If you were Queen. It's the sort of thing Queens say.'

'Often?' asked Michael.

'All the time,' said the Queen.

THE ROYAL CALAMITY (PART ONE)

In the darkest corner of the banqueting hall there was an old, old picture. It was so ancient that its original colours had darkened until it looked as if it had been painted in nothing but shades of brown. It had hung in its corner for hundreds of years and generations of Ladies-in-Waiting had begged that it should not be removed. They were always afraid that once down it would never be hung up again, and it was their favourite picture. And this was because among its faded shadows it was possible to make out the gloomy outlines of a crowd of ladies. And the enchanting thing about these ladies (to the admirers of the picture) was that they were all wearing glittering tiaras that looked like small crowns. And the picture was plainly labelled, in old fashioned letters,

The Ladies-in-Waiting.

It was the tiaras that really fascinated the Ladies-in-Waiting. They could not get over the

fact that their ancestors had had these ornaments (so like small crowns) while they themselves did not. Luckily the Ladies-in-Waiting had so many other worries that they did not often find time to brood upon their missing adornments, but every so often they would remember, and go and stare wistfully at the picture in the banqueting hall, and then they would petition the Queen to provide them with the embellishments (if not small crowns) their dignity demanded.

But the Queen never would. She said that the Ladies-in-Waiting were bad enough with hairnets and blue rinses, never mind tiaras and she threatened to have the picture taken away. Then the Ladies-in-Waiting would become sensitive and peevish and dignified, like princesses in exile.

It was while the Ladies-in-Waiting were at their most peevish and dignified that the Queen invited everyone in the palace (except the Cook) to come and take turns on the Royal Slide.

The Royal Slide was half a mile long. It started at the top of the tallest turret and ended in the banqueting hall. It had seven twists, thick silver plating, and had been very expensive to install.

Everyone, especially the Ladies-in-Waiting, was forever hinting that the money it had cost

could have been much better spent (on tiaras, for instance).

After a while the Queen got tired of these remarks and she thought that if she allowed everyone (except, of course, the Cook) to have turns on the slide then they would become as fond of it as she was herself.

(Michael had been allowed on it from the start, and the Royal Donkey would have been too, had he not been a donkey. (But he was a donkey.))

But nobody wanted to go on the slide. (Except, of course, the Cook).

'Ye shameless hussy and me in me kilt!' exclaimed the Treasurer when the invitation arrived and the Queen was forced to agree that he had a point.

'Alas, I have not the figure,' said the Prime Minister's wife, and the Queen reluctantly admitted that this was perfectly true. The Prime Minister did make several descents from the heights, (arranged by the Queen who conducted him to the top and then shouted 'SIT DOWN' at a suitable moment). But the Prime Minister never appeared to notice at all that anything had happened and so it was completely wasted on him.

The Ladies-in-Waiting flatly refused to go, because of their unadorned dignity and the Cook said, 'Why wasn't I asked?'

'Because,' the Queen told her, 'You are too fa ...' and then she suddenly remembered that it was not good policy to quarrel with the Cook and said instead, 'Because the slide is too thin.'

'Too thin my foot!' exclaimed the Cook, enormously offended despite the Queen's tactfulness, and she marched down to the kitchen and gazed at her reflection in the bottom of a frying pan saying,

'Fancy! The Cheek! What I am expected to endure! Saints would not put up with what I put up with in this dratted hole of a palace!' And similar comforting remarks.

Now when the Ladies-in-Waiting were in their
Exiled-Princesses sort of mood they took even
more than their usual delight in being annoying.
And it occurred to them that it would amuse their
exiled dignity to see the Cook on the slide,
especially as the slide was so thin in comparison
with the width of the Cook. So when the Queen
was out of the way visiting the Royal Donkey they
went to the kitchen and remarked to the Cook
that she was indeed put upon. And what a cheek
the Queen had implying she was less wide than
the slide, when anyone could see she was slender
as slender. Also they said that if they were as
young as she they would slide all day (and since
none of them would admit to being a day over
seventeen (and many had stuck firmly to this
policy for twenty or thirty years) this was
amazingly flattering to the Cook). And with many

other comments of this kind they coaxed the Cook to climb the highest turret and sat her down on the top of the slide, and with the gentle dignity of those who should by rights be crowned (or at least have tiaras), they gave her an enormous shove.

The Cook travelled about fifty yards and then stuck.

No amount of encouragement or advice or ridicule could shift her.

The Ladies-in-Waiting grew quite desperate and the poor Cook grew very desperate because of a strange swelling feeling that was growing in her from the waist down. She called the Ladies-in-Waiting frightful names and said they would catch it when the Queen came back.

'She will guess you was behind it,' said the Cook and her listeners realised that this was true and that the Queen would know straight away that nothing except several dozen Ladies-in-Waiting pushing from behind could have got the Cook up the dozens of winding stairs that led to the top of the highest turret.

Everyone thought and thought in dignified panic and the thought that gradually drifted into their heads was that some form of lubrication was needed.

'What about oil?' they called down to the Cook.

'Nasty foreign muck,' said the Cook. 'Makes the

lettuce greasy! But you might try butter!'

'Butter?' repeated the Ladies-in-Waiting and the Cook said yes, best butter and they need not try fobbing her off with some low fat marg as it had no strength in it. The Ladies-in-Waiting quite agreed that strength was what was needed and they fetched several pounds of best butter from the kitchen and shot them down to the Cook.

After that there followed several minutes of desperate writhing and then the Cook positioned herself above the butter and pushed off as hard as she could and slid slowly down to the banqueting hall. She arrived slightly squashed and thoroughly buttered but otherwise unhurt.

For various reasons nobody mentioned any of this to the Queen.

Unfortunately, the very next morning the Queen decided that it would be more interesting to arrive at breakfast by way of her slide, rather than

 boringly
through the
banqueting hall
door, and so she
climbed up to
the top of the
tallest turret

and sat down and pushed herself off and after fifty
yards she hit the Cook's butter at very high speed.

Then things happened terribly quickly.

The Queen flashed along that half mile of silver
slide so fast she did not notice its seven twists at
all.

She did not even notice the butter. It was like
dropping down a shaft of light. Nor did she stop
when she reached the end. She shot off the
bottom of the slide and flew in a graceful arc
across the width of the banqueting hall,
considerably startling the Prime Minister's wife
and the Treasurer and the Ladies-in-Waiting who

were eating their breakfast beneath. She hit the opposite wall at a height of about fifteen feet and a speed of about twenty-five miles an hour and it was at this point that she came to a halt.

'Why are we eating this horrible low fat spread?' enquired the Prime Minister peevishly.

'I much prefer butter.'

But nobody ever replied. They had noticed what he had not: the Queen lying flat on her back on the floor of the banqueting hall bellowing,

'OH MY FOOT! OH MY POOR FOOT! OH MY POOR, POOR FOOT!'

They perceived that something was wrong. And so it was. The Queen's ankle was broken.

'It CAN'T be!' exclaimed the Queen when the Royal Doctor imparted this horrible news. 'I am QUEEN!'

The Royal Doctor replied that even Queens could not collide with stone walls feet first at twenty-five miles an hour and not suffer any inconvenience, and he bound up the Queen's foot with bandages and plaster, wrote out a prescription for two crutches, warned her that it would probably be agony but on no account to call him out in the middle of the night, and hurried back to his golf.

Even now, for various reasons, nobody had mentioned the events of the previous afternoon to the Queen. Unfortunately, when she was being carried to the sofa the Prime Minister suddenly caught sight of her back view and exclaimed, 'Oh there's the butter!'

And then the cat was out of the bag and there was nothing to do but explain.

The Queen did not take the news well.

On the contrary, she was hopping (literally) mad.

She told the Cook what she thought of her, and it was terrible, and she told the Ladies-in-Waiting, and it was infinitely worse, and she pointed out that in the good old days they would have been severely punished (to the point of execution) for what they had done. Also for several nights running she forced the Ladies-in-Waiting to call out the Royal Doctor. And what the Royal Doctor said to them in consequence was so unkind that they almost wished they were back in the good old days of execution-and-be-done-with-it. All in all, it was not a happy time for the Ladies-in-Waiting. They were organised into two shifts, and when one shift was looking after the Queen (who was not a patient patient) the other was cleaning the butter-covered slide. And to do this the Ladies-in-Waiting climbed up to the tallest turret, seated themselves on piles of old dusters, and then gingerly, inch by inch, made their way along its half mile of treacherous length to the end. And then they climbed up the dozens of winding stairs and did it again. This had been Michael's idea. It was far from good for the Ladies-in-Waiting's dignity, but it cheered up the Queen tremendously to watch.

THE ROYAL CALAMITY (PART TWO)

After the first few days of agony the Queen's
broken ankle got well enough for her to hobble
about on crutches. But that was all she could do,
hobble rather slowly, taking great care not to
accidentally bump her foot against chairs or
thrones or Ladies-in-Waiting, because that
brought the agony back as fiercely as if it had
never been away. Whenever this happened, and
the Queen howled and groaned in consequence,
the Ladies-in-Waiting said What A Fuss About A
Little Bump and Wait Till Something Really Bad

Happens To You and they advised her to sit down and be quiet and remember some people would like a little peace. The Queen thought they were probably the worst nurses in the world and she told them so.

'Charming!' said the Ladies-in-Waiting. 'After all our trouble!'

'Your trouble!' said the Queen. 'It's me that's got the broken ankle!'

'Next you'll be saying it's our fault,' replied the Ladies-in-Waiting.

'OF COURSE it's your fault!' answered the astonished Queen. 'You buttered the Cook!'

'Unfortunately it was the only thing to do under the circumstances,' replied the Ladies-in-Waiting with dignity, 'and, incidentally, we still have not been thanked.'

'Thanked!' said the Queen bitterly.

'Or rewarded in any way,' continued the Ladies-in-Waiting, staring very meaningfully at the tiara picture.

'Rewarded!' repeated the Queen. 'Rewarded for buttering the Cook! Why ever didn't you leave her where she was? She would have come loose in the end. She only needed to thin down a bit and she would have slid down naturally.'

'It would have taken weeks,' replied the Ladies-in-Waiting scornfully. 'We did the only sensible thing.'

The Queen said that the sensible thing would have been to leave the Cook in the kitchen where she belonged, and the Ladies-in-Waiting asked if they were to be blamed for desiring a little innocent diversion to cheer lives otherwise blighted with injustice and disappointment. Which meant, in plain speech, We shall do as we like because we haven't got tiaras. And whose fault is it that we haven't?

'Tiaras?' said Michael, coming in with his usual

suddenness and at once guessing the thoughts of the Ladies-in-Waiting (who were again gazing at their picture). 'Tiaras! If you ask me they don't deserve heads, never mind tiaras! If I were you I would take that picture down. It is addling their brains. How's your foot today?'

'Bored,' replied the Queen gloomily, who ever since the moment that her ankle had snapped had longed to be tree climbing or donkey racing or tobogganing down hills. 'Bored, and it's spreading up my leg to my head.'

'Never mind,' said Michael, standing a small table on the sideboard beneath the tiara picture and balancing a stool on the top. 'I've been looking in the library for interesting things to do on crutches. I'll tell you about it in a minute. I'll just get this thing down for you first.'

'This is too cruel!' sobbed the Ladies-in-Waiting.

'Sometimes you have to be cruel to be kind,'

said Michael cheerfully as he climbed on to the stool. 'Once your brain is addled, it's addled! You will thank us for it in the end!'

And the Queen said What a Fuss About An Old Picture and Wait Till Something Really Bad Happens To You and would they try to remember

that some people would like a little peace. So the Ladies-in-Waiting left in outraged dignity to snuffle in their bedrooms and the Queen felt happier than she had done for days.

'The thing I discovered,' said Michael, as he dusted sheets of black cobwebs off the back of the picture and slid it out of sight behind the sideboard, 'that seems to be what everyone does with crutches, is to look for buried treasure.'

'Buried treasure?' asked the Queen.

'That's what they do in books.'

'What sort of books?'

'Pirate books,' said Michael. 'Pirates hardly ever have more than one good leg and they look for buried treasure all over the place. Even on desert islands.'

'Do they find it?' enquired the Queen with interest.

'Always,' said Michael.

This was a very cheering suggestion, especially

to someone who lived, not on a desert island (where hardly anyone rich must ever go), but in a palace where generations of wealthy Kings and Queens had wandered about the gardens burying goodness-knows-what.

'We're bound to find something,' said Michael, 'even if it isn't exactly treasure.'

'Bones,' said the Queen.

'Heads!' said Michael.

'Ladies-in-Waiting's heads!' said the Queen.

'Buried in a box!' said Michael.

'Because my ancestors got so tired of them!' said the Queen. 'You could chop off heads in those days,' she added rather wistfully.

'Never mind,' said Michael comfortingly. 'Let's go and start digging.'

After that for days and days the Queen and Michael searched for buried treasure, or bones, or Ladies-in-Waiting's heads in a box. They dug in every likely place; at the base of sundials and the foot of ancient trees, at the tops of humps and the bottoms of hollows and in the middle of the maze (where they found the Prime Minister who had been mislaid for days). The Queen chose the places where they were to search and Michael (who was a gardener's boy by profession and so very good with a spade) did the actual digging. (They did not have to dig for the Prime Minister. He was lying on the top of the ground, alive but bemused. (He went back to work immediately.))

While all this digging was in progress the Ladies-in-Waiting were having serious thoughts about how wise it had been to butter the Royal Slide and then tell the Queen that it was her fault that she had broken her ankle on it. The Cook, when she heard the story, had been far from sympathetic.

'About time that 'orrible picture come down,' she said. 'I should have had it off the wall years ago. It did nothing but encourage you with your airs and graces and highfalutin' sighing and pining and never a stroke of work done from dawn to dusk among the lot of you!'

'But ...' began the Ladies-in-Waiting.

'You're none of you no better than you ought to be,' continued the Cook (who had not yet forgiven them for the incident on the slide), 'and why we should have to put up with you simpering and whimpering because some silly picture painter drew you all with crowns on is more than I can understand ...'

'Tiaras,' murmured the Ladies-in-Waiting faintly.

'Tiaras,' said the Cook contemptuously. 'Hairnets and moustaches would have been more like it, but you'll not see it again and a good thing too. The Queen has put her foot down and that young rip Michael is backing her up. You'll need to put some work in before you charm that picture back on to the wall again!'

The Ladies-in-Waiting reeled out of the kitchen, absolutely shattered by so much straight talking all at one go, but the phrase, 'Charm that picture back on to the wall,' stuck in their heads.

They couldn't help wondering if it would be possible to do such a thing.

'Anyway,' they told each other, 'it is worth a try.'

So, much to the Queen's surprise, they suddenly began to ask her how she felt, and to take an interest in the treasure hunting, enquiring in kindly (if condescending) voices whether she had had any luck that day.

'Not yet,' the Queen always answered, 'but I expect we shall soon.'

Then the Ladies-in-Waiting would look amused and disbelieving and reply, 'Of course you will Your Majesty,' and stare charmingly up at the empty patch of wall where their picture had been.

The Queen thought that treasure hunting was very good fun, whether they found anything or not. Everyday she could hop faster and further on her crutches and her ankle got more and more solid and dependable feeling. Often the Royal Donkey came with them, and when it was his turn to choose where to dig he would always walk straight to the kitchen gardens where the carrots were planted.

'He is very intelligent,' said the Queen affectionately. 'What would you rather find Michael, treasure or Ladies-in-Waiting's heads in a box?'

'Oh, I just like digging,' said Michael cheerfully.
'What would you rather find yourself?'

'I can never choose,' said the Queen dreamily.

Meanwhile the Ladies-in-Waiting realised that
they were not having much success in charming
their picture back on to the wall and they renewed
their efforts to take an intelligent interest in the
Queen's new occupation.

'What, exactly, are you looking for?' they asked.

'Oh, just any old treasure,' replied the Queen,
politely not mentioning the Ladies-in-Waiting's
heads in a box, which she and Michael continually
pretended to each other they had just discovered.
'Any old treasure, gold and jewels and stuff.'

The Ladies-in-Waiting simpered charmingly
and said they expected it was just a matter of time.
They really were trying very hard. They even took
to suggesting places where they thought the
Queen and Michael might dig, to show that they

believed it was possible that they actually might find treasure. Gradually, as time went on, their pretended interest became quite real. 'Perhaps,' they told each other idly, 'perhaps, perhaps ...' After all, the Queen had an astonishing knack of getting her own way. Look how that donkey had won the Royal Horse Race.

One day Michael's spade struck something very solid with a sort of clunking sound.

'It feels like wood,' he told the Queen.

'Have we found it? Have we found it?' asked the Queen excitedly, hopping around on her crutches and nearly falling into the hole. 'Scrape, Michael, scrape!'

Michael scraped and paused, and scraped again.

'Sorry,' he said after a moment. 'I thought it was a box but it's just a piece of plank,' and he bent down and picked it up, and passed it to the Queen.

'It's got writing on it,' she said, after inspecting it for a minute. 'It says DIG something.'

'Dig here?' asked Michael eagerly.

'Hang on,' said the Queen busy rubbing with the hem of her cloak, 'I've nearly got it clean. Oh.'

'What?'

'DIG NO FURTHER. That's what it says.'

'Shall I stop then?' asked Michael.

'Definitely not,' said the Queen.

The next bit of wood that Michael unearthed said:

NOTHING GOOD WILL COME OF THIS

and the next bit cautioned:

DON'T SAY YOU HAVEN'T BEEN WARNED

'Hmmm,' said Michael.

'It can't be,' said the Queen.

The next thing to appear was not a bit of wood, but the lid of a box.

'Oh Michael!' whispered the Queen, because

when the box was lifted out of the hole it could be seen that a large crown was carved on the lid, and underneath, in deep black letters,

REMOVED, BY ORDER OF THE MONARCH

The box was very securely fastened, which was rather a relief for the Queen. For the first time in all their happy treasure hunting days she and Michael did not joke about what they might discover as an alternative to gold. Instead they stared at one another, quite pale with shock.

'We could put it back,' said the Queen at last, 'but then we would never stop wondering. Wondering might be worse than knowing. You can wonder such a lot when it's dark and you really get going.' And she stared thoughtfully at the piece of wood which remarked,

DON'T SAY YOU HAVEN'T BEEN WARNED

'Anyway,' said Michael, taking courage. 'It's not

big enough to hold a whole Lady-in-Waiting, that's one thing.'

'We shall have to look now we've found it,' decided the Queen bravely, 'but not here, with it getting dark and so many worms about. Let's take it back to the palace.'

'Perhaps the Cook ...' suggested Michael.

'Yes, perhaps the Cook,' agreed the Queen eagerly. 'She must be used to all sorts of terrible sights, cooking! I'm sure she wouldn't mind. And if it's treasure we'll give her a bit. And if it isn't, we'll know. And we can put it back. With stronger warnings this time.'

So the Queen and Michael staggered back to the palace with the box and dumped it on the kitchen floor and explained to the Cook what they thought it might contain (although it might possibly be treasure). And the Cook cheerfully agreed to open the box and look, on the understanding that if it was, after all, treasure she would be allowed to keep a bit, and if it wasn't, then she should be the one to break the news of its contents to the present Ladies-in-Waiting. The Cook seemed to regard this by way of being a treat.

So with the rolling pin and the help of several tin openers the locks were prized apart, and then Michael and the Queen took deep breaths and looked anywhere but at the box and the Cook

threw back the lid. And then the Queen and Michael heard a terrible groaning gasp.

'My Sainted Soul!' exclaimed the Cook hoarsely, as the lid crashed shut again. 'Oh, that gave me such a turn! Oh, I must have a drop or else I shall expire! Oh, I haven't had such a shock since the Butcher last came!'

She really did look terribly ill. Michael hurried to prop her comfortably against the table while the Queen fetched the cooking rum and poured a large dose.

'You get that thing out of here!' said the Cook after the first mugful had gone down and she had begun to feel better. 'Oh, it made my blood run cold! If them Ladies-in-Waiting see what's in that box they will never be the same again and it's us as will have to live with them. It will do for their heads sure as fate. They're weak witted enough as it is!'

'But what exactly ...?' asked Michael. 'Oh!'

For the Cook had opened the box again and pointed a shaking finger at the awful, gleaming contents, brighter and more dreadful than anything he or the Queen had ever imagined.

'Cooee!' called a voice down the stairs. 'We saw you come in, Your Majesty, with your lovely exciting black box!'

'Get it out of here!' ordered the Cook. 'Nothing good will come of it! Don't say you haven't been warned! Quick, while I distract them. Whatever can I do?'

'Nail up that picture!' said the Queen, suddenly inspired. 'It's still behind the sideboard where Michael pushed it! Nail it up crooked and let them help you to get it straight and while you're doing it Michael and I will ...'

But Michael had already picked up his spade.

Never had the Ladies-in-Waiting known such a victory. The Cook balanced on the sideboard rehanging their picture by Royal Command. With every blow of the hammer their triumph increased. They were distracted, enchanted and bewildered by their sudden good fortune. And what was the Cook mumbling through her mouthful of nails? They strained their elegant ears to listen.

'Never thought I should live to see the day. Charmed it on to the wall you have and I must eat my words. Well, quality will out and no mistake and I don't doubt that if there was any justice you'd all be ...'

The Cook suddenly choked on a nail.

'Crowned?' suggested a Lady-in-Waiting softly.

'Ah well,' said the Cook.

They grew more and more gracious. They said, magnificently, 'Sorry about that little affair on the slide Cook. Our mistake. Underestimated you.'

It was ages and ages before they remembered the box they had seen carried to the kitchen by Michael and the Queen.

'Treasure?' they asked, smiling indulgently, knowing it wasn't.

'Junk,' said the Cook, rising superbly to the occasion. 'Mucky old ironmongery chucked out and buried. "You can get that out of my clean kitchen," I said. "Back where you got it from and double quick too!" You got to stand up for your rights in this place!'

The Ladies-in-Waiting nodded in kindly agreement.

'Dear old Cook,' they thought. 'So vulgar!'

Outside in the dark Michael and the Queen were congratulating each other.

'Twice as deep and stamped down hard!' said Michael. 'Gosh! What if they'd got their hands on them!'

'Heads on them,' said the Queen.

'Heads under them,' said Michael.

'Just imagine,' said the Queen, 'if we'd walked in

with the box and dumped it in the banqueting hall and said "There's your tiaras!" What would they do?'

'I'm not digging them up again,' said Michael firmly.

'Of course not,' said the Queen. 'I was just wondering. You can wonder such a lot when it's dark and you really get going.'

POLAR BEARS ARE VERY HARD TO TAME (AND OTHER PROBLEMS)

The Queen's broken ankle was almost completely better when the Get Well presents began to arrive. This was partly the Prime Minister's fault. When the news of the Royal Accident had first been announced Reigning Monarchs from all over the world had written to him to ask what the Queen would like as a present to cheer her up, and the Prime Minister (after much anxious thought) had written back:

Dear Sir or Madam,
I really could not say.
Yours truly,
The Prime Minister.
P.S. She likes the Royal Donkey.

Naturally enough, the Reigning Monarchs
(mostly Foreign Princes but with a scattering of
Kings and Queens) had taken this to be a polite
hint that some form of livestock would be
appreciated. So livestock was what they sent, and
not any old livestock either. No Reigning
Monarch worth his crown would send anything
but the best to a fellow Reigning Monarch. The
animals that were dispatched by the Kings and
Queens (but mostly Foreign Princes) were the
most spectacular available in their distant lands.

But not necessarily the most convenient.

Day after day they arrived at the palace, all
neatly labelled:

c/o The Prime Minister, with kindest regards to The Queen.

HANDLE WITH CARE

It was the Prime Minister's job to unwrap them and to write the thank-you letters, and very soon he began to dread the arrival of the post.

At first it was not too bad. Thirty-four guinea pigs squashed into a very small crate.

('I do quite like guinea pigs,' said the Queen).

'Thank you very much for all those lovely guinea pigs,' the Prime Minister wrote to South America.

'I only sent two,' said the letter that came back.

The Prime Minister was so sure that there had

been more than two that he went out and counted them again and there were one hundred and forty six.

'Most peculiar,' he thought, but he did not mention it to anyone. He was tired of people criticising his maths, and besides, he had other worries. An enormous parcel had arrived from the Snowy North, wrapped in sheet steel and packed in ice and smelling very strongly of fish. It contained two polar bears and no instructions.

'I can't think what we are to use them for,' said the Queen, watching from a safe distance while the Prime Minister very gingerly examined the labels tied around their necks. 'Unless they are very, very tame. They will make brilliant draft excluders if they are. I think it is quite important to find out.'

The Prime Minister completely agreed, and he wrote at once to the Snowy North a letter which said,

'URGENT! MOST IMPORTANT! ARE THEY TAME? OR NOT?'

And after ages and ages he received a very laconic reply which stated,

'Well, not, actually.

P.S. Polar bears are very hard to tame.'

The sender of the tigers was a lot more helpful and replied to the Prime Minister's quite frantic thank-you letter at once.

'We were so pleased to hear the tigers arrived

safely. As long as they are treated with great caution and kindness and given an abundant diet there should be no cause for alarm.

P.S. I should think the same would apply to the polar bears.

P.P.S. And the lions.'

'What lions?' asked the Queen, and at that very moment the lions arrived. Almost from the beginning they seemed to hate the tigers.

'The lions have come,' wrote the Prime Minister with feverish haste (the roaring and prowlings in the shrubbery at night were appalling). 'Please advise re. control in the presence of tigers.'

No reply ever came to this letter, nor to the one about the wolves, or the one about the elephant seals (strange animals, as big as elephants and shaped like seals and very hot tempered).

'I always thought Get Well presents were chocolates and flowers and bubble bath,' remarked the Queen. 'Why do you think I never get anything like that?'

'I really couldn't imagine,' said the Prime Minister, who never could imagine anything.

More post arrived: pandas, grizzly bears, two camels and a yak. The pandas, although beautiful, were terribly fussy eaters and never seemed to enjoy anything unless it was bamboo shoots flown

in at enormous expense from China. The grizzly
bears, on the other hand, were terribly unfussy
eaters and consumed anything, including (to the
Prime Minister's secret relief) all except two of the
guinea pigs. There were other problems as well;
the camels continually wandered off, and the yak
fell in love with the Cook and insisted on
following her round the kitchen, moulting

everywhere so that food acquired a chewy, woolly sort of feeling in the mouth that was very unpopular. The Himalayan Prince who had dispatched the yak was no help at all.

'Yaks,' he wrote proudly, 'are noble, loyal beasts. They are impossible to distract and fall in love for life.'

'Thank you very much,' said the Cook bitterly, when the Prime Minister showed her this letter. 'How long do they live for?'

'I don't know,' said the Prime Minister. 'All I know is I can't cope with this much longer. I have writer's cramp and my nerves are in shreds, my wife refuses to help, and as for the Ladies-in-Waiting ...'

'Impertinent young madams!' interrupted the Cook, who had had to endure a great deal from the Ladies-in-Waiting on the subject of the love-struck yak.

'Precisely,' said the Prime Minister. ' "We fail to

see your problem Prime Minister," they say to me,
"Do you wish us to recount the guinea pigs for
you? Why not call a General Election if you feel
you can't cope!" And the Queen worries about
nothing but that ridiculous donkey and no one
shows the slightest bit of concern for my bites!'

'Camel?' enquired the Cook with interest.
'Tiger?'

'No, no,' said the Prime Minister, scratching
peevishly. 'Much smaller.'

'Guinea pigs?' asked the Cook.

'They may have jumped off the guinea pigs,'
admitted the Prime Minister. 'I really couldn't say.
But I know for certain that I am close to being
eaten alive!'

He was not the only one. At that moment a
streaking blur of lions and tigers hurtled past the
kitchen window, united for once in common
pursuit of the Royal Donkey. Seconds later the
door was flung open, the Queen and the donkey

shot in, slammed it shut, and collapsed panting to
the floor.

'That settles it!' said the Queen, as soon as she
had breath enough to speak. 'Those Get Well
presents are all going back where they came from!
Goodness knows what would have happened if I
hadn't thought to distract them!'

It wasn't hard to guess. From the other side of
the kitchen door came a terrible crunching of
crutches.

'Not very nice,' continued the Queen, listening while she stroked flat the donkey's fur, every hair of which was standing on end with surprise. 'Not very nice at all! They must definitely go, and the sooner the better!'

'Can you send them back?' enquired the Prime Minister. 'After all, they were presents. It is hardly polite! What about the international situation?'

'What about the Royal Donkey?' replied the Queen. 'Bother the international situation! No, they must all go at once. I shall pretend I thought they were loans instead of presents. The Prime Minister can start packing them up straight away.'

'How shall I know where to send them?' asked the Prime Minister.

'By the labels of course,' replied the Queen. 'And I shall send a Lady-in-Waiting back with each animal to take care of it on the journey. A change of air will do the Ladies-in-Waiting good. They are always saying they don't get out enough.'

The Cook and the Prime Minister agreed that this was an excellent idea. The Cook began making sandwiches at once for the journeys, while the Prime Minister began another batch of letters.

'Dear Sir or Madam,

Thank you very much for the loan of your lovely animals. Our foot is quite better now so we are sending them back.

P.S. I am also sending a Lady-in-Waiting to look after them.

P.P.S. Please feel free to keep the Lady-in-Waiting (enclosed) if it would give you pleasure.'

After that the returning of the Get Well presents began in earnest. Unfortunately, many of them seemed to have misplaced their labels and so the Prime Minister had to be shut up in the library with a lot of encyclopedias and maps until he managed to trace the native home of each animal.

On the whole he did this surprisingly well.
Research, he called it, and took it very seriously,
carefully comparing the pictures in the books with
the actual live presents. He was very puzzled at
first by the fact that many of the animals appeared
to have twice as many legs as those shown in the
encyclopedia, but he got on quite well once it was
explained to him that the missing legs were
concealed behind the visible legs, thus:

As soon as it was discovered where an animal belonged it was dispatched with its accompanying Lady-in-Waiting, waved off from the station by the Queen. And some of the Ladies-in-Waiting were agog with excitement at the thought of being kept at the pleasure of Foreign Princes, and some were resentful, and some feverishly read and reread the instructions about kindness and caution and an abundant diet as if their lives depended on it.

But eventually they were all gone, animals and Ladies-in-Waiting as well, and for a while the palace was very peaceful.

It didn't last long however. In dribs and drabs the Ladies-in-Waiting began to return, and some had frostbite and some had sunstroke and they were all very lean and brown and offended. And eventually the palace was full again and even the two who had been sent to the wrong ends of the world (because the Prime Minister had confused polar bears with pandas (a very easy mistake to make)) arrived home.

But one Lady-in-Waiting never came back. And the Queen (who was a kind Queen) always hoped it was because she was being kept with pleasure by a handsome Foreign Prince. It was the fat one who had been sent with the tigers.

GYPSY FORTUNES

It was an autumn afternoon; cool blue air, thick damp grass, and an emptiness in the sky where the swallows had been. The rustle of the brown and gold and crimson leaves twirling down from the trees was the only sound to be heard.

Michael, the Queen's best friend, had unexpectedly announced that he supposed it was time he saw the world. And he had gone off to see it, without mentioning why he had decided to go, or whether he was sorry to leave, or when (if ever) he intended to come back.

This was surprisingly awful for the Queen; she found all at once that she had no one to talk to. Nobody in the palace seemed to want to listen to anything she had to say. They were not at all interested in hearing about Michael (who had gone away so suddenly), or the Royal Donkey, or what the Queen thought about all the things she thought about. They wriggled and yawned and blinked their eyes so slowly that it seemed that they would never open them again. Eventually the Queen gave up and trudged across to the stables to talk to the donkey instead. She felt very lonely.

Everyone in the palace sighed with relief and slumped back down to their dozing; but no sooner were their eyes safely shut than they were jerked awake again. The waiting autumn afternoon was suddenly filled with the rattle of wheels and the barking of dogs, the clatter of hooves, and voices calling. Painted caravans, bright as flowers, were rolling up the drive. It was the Wraggle Taggle

Gypsies, come to see the Queen.

'She's out!' the Ladies-in-Waiting told the
gypsies, sniffing in disgust at the sight of people
so unlike themselves. 'She's gone off with that
donkey! Goodbye! Close the gate! Round the back

next time please! We'll tell her you called if you think it matters.'

'Of course it matters!' said the brightest and most ragged of all the gypsies. 'Was there ever a fortune that didn't matter?'

'Fortunes!' exclaimed the Ladies-in-Waiting, suddenly waking up. They crowded eagerly round the gypsy girl, pushing and squabbling in their hurry to cross her palms with gold and silver and have their fortunes told.

But when they heard their fortunes they were not pleased. 'Be off with you!' they said to the laughing gypsies. 'We didn't pay good gold and silver to listen to fortunes like that!'

'Your fortunes are your fortunes,' replied the gypsies cheerfully, 'and gold and silver are the least of it! And don't forget to tell the Queen we called!'

But nobody passed on the gypsies' message to the Queen. It was night when she came home and morning when she found out what had happened, and it was the Cook who told her because the Ladies-in-Waiting were all lying face down on their beds gloomily brooding over their awful fortunes and refusing to get up.

'What ever is the matter with them all?' asked the Queen.

'The Wraggle Taggle Gypsies is the matter,' said the Cook. 'Turned up yesterday afternoon and told them fortunes they didn't care for!'

'The Wraggle Taggle Gypsies!' exclaimed the Queen. 'Oh, where are they now?'

'Sent packing,' said the Cook carelessly, 'They was seen off the premises, fortunes and all. They'll be long gone by now. Over the hills and far away I shouldn't wonder!'

Suddenly the thought of another day surrounded by Ladies-in-Waiting and with no one to talk to was too much for the Queen. She ran to the stables where the Cook would not see her tears and between hiccups she told the Royal Donkey that the Wraggle Taggle Gypsies had come and gone, over the hills and far away, and that once again she had been left behind, and she could bear it no longer.

The Royal Donkey waited until the worst of the hiccups was over and then he took the Queen very gently by the scruff of the neck and led her to the edge of the meadow where the fallen leaves had drifted on to the shaggy autumn grass. Face up on the golden leaves was a silver coin with the Queen's head showing.

The second coin was gold to show up on the white chalky road that ran through the woods from the meadow, and the third coin was silver on the golden lichen of a stile. The fourth was gold on the white flag stepping stones that crossed the stream at the foot of the hill. And the fifth was silver on the bracken at the top.

Silver on gold, and gold on silver led the trail, all the silver and gold of the Ladies-in-Waiting's fortunes, and always turned face up like an invitation. Over the hills and far away it led the Queen and the Royal Donkey, until suddenly they smelt a whiff of wood smoke in the air and came to a clearing in the middle of a beech wood, and there, all at once, was the gypsies' camp.

In no time at all a circle of people had surrounded them, and a gypsy girl (the brightest and raggediest and dustiest of them all) stepped

forward and held out her hand. 'Hello,' she said.

'Hello,' said the Queen, and they looked at
each other in admiration. The gypsy girl's hair was
tangled brown and the Queen's was tangled gold,
and the gypsy girl's eyes were shining black while

the Queen's were shining blue, but apart from that they were very alike. Their clothes were equally bright and almost equally torn (the Queen's had more tears but the gypsy girl's had more patches). Gold bracelets on the Queen and gold earrings on the gypsy girl flashed in the sunlight as they smiled at one another, and over both was an equally thick layer of fine white dust from the chalky roads.

'You must be the Queen,' said the gypsy girl.

'And so must you,' said the Queen, because she had never before seen anyone who looked so like herself.

The gypsies laughed.

'We're all Queens here,' they told her, 'or Kings or Princes or Princesses or Emperors, or at least have empty pockets.'

'Empty pockets?' asked the Queen.

'What about all that gold and silver you passed to find us?' they said. 'Where is it?'

'Where it was,' said the Queen, surprised.

'That's how we knew who you were,' said the gypsy girl. 'We could tell at once. Only a Queen would have left it where it was and come along with empty pockets. Anyone else would have picked it up and spent it and never arrived, or picked it up and kept it and we'd have heard the jingle in their pockets and been gone before they got here. You're just in time for breakfast! Are you hungry?'

'Dreadfully,' said the Queen.

Breakfast was roast pheasant and mushrooms, and lunch was poached salmon and raspberries. And tea was pancakes with honey and cream. In between meals the Queen talked and talked, and the gypsies listened and listened. And she told them all about the Royal Donkey, and all about Michael (who had so suddenly gone away) and about all the things she thought about. And at the end of the telling the Queen had an empty, peaceful, happy feeling, and she knew that when she went back to the palace she would be her old self again, perfectly able to cope alone even with the Ladies-in-Waiting until Michael got back.

'I suppose I'd better go back to the palace,' she said reluctantly at the end of the day. 'It has been nice!'

'You look out for us again,' said the gypsies. 'We're always about, somewhere or other.'

'Did you know I was coming today?' asked the Queen curiously.

'It was a fair guess,' replied the gypsies. 'Those Ladies-in-Waiting would be enough to make anyone take to the woods!' And they added that she was not the first to slip out of a palace to go in search of the gypsies.

'Many a lady,' they said, 'and many a Queen. There's more ways than one of seeking your fortune!'

'Would you like to come back with me?' asked

the Queen.

'No, no,' said the gypsies, shaking their heads. 'Thanking you kindly, but we'll be moving straight on in the morning.'

'If I were you,' said the Queen, looking at the purple autumn sky and the falling gold of the leaves of the beech trees. 'I'd stay here for ever! And then I could always find you.'

'If you were us,' said the gypsy girl, laughing, 'you'd move straight on in the morning, because that's what gypsies do. But don't worry; you'll see us again. Straight on always comes back in the end.'

'Next time you come to the palace there'll be pheasant and mushrooms for breakfast, and salmon and raspberries for lunch, and pancakes and honey and cream for tea, and perhaps Michael will be there,' promised the Queen. 'But I thought you said you never go back.'

'Going back and coming back are two different

'things,' the gypsies told her.

'Are they?'

'Always,' said the gypsies, and they piled her with presents. A lovely fortune and a basket of blackberries. A striped lurcher pup. A cold roast chicken to eat on the way home, and a dozen red apples with a large spotted handkerchief to carry them in. A necklace of rosehips and a straw hat for the donkey to keep the dust from his eyes. And the brightest and raggediest of them all, the gypsy girl, gave the Queen her own golden earrings with

dangling bells. Then they waved her goodbye, and she set off back to the palace, very tired, very dusty, very happy, and with empty pockets.

'Where have you been?' demanded the Ladies-in-Waiting.

'Over the hills and far away,' said the Queen, kicking off her dusty boots and climbing into bed. 'And I found the gypsies and they told me my fortune.'

'Gypsy fortunes!' sniffed the Ladies-in-Waiting. 'Dreadful old tales! They make them up!'

'Of course they do,' said the Queen sleepily. 'Mine was lovely!'

'Fancy believing gypsy fortunes!' said the Ladies-in-Waiting to each other, but they said it less and less confidently as the days went by and their gypsy fortunes became more and more dismally and accurately true.

'Perhaps you could find the gypsies and ask for something better,' suggested the Queen, and the

Ladies-in-Waiting thought this was a good idea.

After that the Queen often met them, searching (quite desperately) the meadows around the palace.

'They're coming back one day,' she promised, 'One spring afternoon ...'

'One day!' said the Ladies-in-Waiting. 'We need them now!' And one of them exclaimed, 'Oh look!'

'What?' said the Queen.

'A silver penny!' said the Lady-in-Waiting, and pounced and picked it up.

That afternoon the Queen found the gypsies again. It was springtime; the woods were green and the sky was silver, there were millions of dandelions and the swallows had come back.

'The Ladies-in-Waiting have been looking for you all winter,' she told the gypsy girl.

'They won't find us though,' the gypsy girl replied. 'They're far too greedy to ever arrive with empty pockets. I don't suppose they'll ever change their fortunes. And speaking of fortunes, how is your own?'

'Quite all right,' said the Queen. 'All of a sudden! Will you come to the palace tomorrow? And stay for breakfast and lunch and tea and meet Michael?'

'I thought he'd gone to see the world!'

'He's seen it,' said the Queen. 'Not all of it, but quite large patches. And he wrote to say it was horrible leaving and he couldn't think why he had decided to go ...'

'Oh?' said the gypsy girl.

'And he's coming straight back in the morning,' said the Queen happily.

HAPPY EVER AFTER

In the palace a most secret and important meeting was in progress. The Queen did not know it was happening, and so that she should not suspect anything it was being held after her bedtime (which was very late) and the Prime Minister had been sent to guard her until she fell asleep. He absolutely astonished the Queen by sticking his head round the Royal Bedroom door and offering to read her a story.

'Read me a story???' asked the Queen. 'Do you know how?'

'Of course I know how,' replied the Prime Minister peevishly.

'Was it your idea?'

'Practically,' said the Prime Minister. 'Well, actually it was my wife's but it comes to the same thing.'

'Oh,' said the Queen eloquently. 'Well you'd better do it then! Can I choose anything I like?'

The Prime Minister said that she could and the Queen chose War and Peace.

'It has more than a thousand pages!' protested the Prime Minister turning to the end of the book.

'I hate short stories,' said the Queen. 'Start at the beginning and explain all the long words and don't miss out any of the jokes!'

Very sulkily the Prime Minister began to read. He explained all the long words as well as he could and the Queen laughed so often that he assumed he was missing none of the jokes. He read in his slowest and most boring voice and gradually the Queen stopped laughing and sank deeper and deeper into the pillows and her eyes began to close. With great relief the Prime Minister skipped more than a thousand pages and turned to the end of the book.

'And they all lived happily ever after!' he announced. 'The End!'

'How could they possibly live happily ever after?' demanded the Queen opening her eyes and sitting up suddenly. 'None of those people could possibly live happily ever after!'

'It's a fairy tale,' said the Prime Minister weakly and untruthfully. 'Anything could happen!'

'It's a war story!' said the Queen. 'You've got all mixed up! Start at the beginning and read it again!'

'Oh really!' exclaimed the Prime Minister crossly, 'and I wanted to go to the mee …' He stopped suddenly. 'Bathroom!'

'To the meebathroom?' asked the Queen. 'Where's that?'

'In the banqueting hall,' said the Prime Minister getting flustered and beginning to gabble. 'Most private and secret!'

'Most private and secret what?' demanded the Queen.

'Meeting in the banqueting hall,' said the Prime Minister panicking and losing his wits completely. 'After her bedtime my wife said and I'm to read her a story and keep her quiet because I won't be any use so I read her War and Peace but she woke up!'

'Who?' shouted the Queen.

'You!' said the Prime Minister madly. 'Woke up and found out about the private and secret meeting in the banqueting hall to decide what to do with you! It didn't work; I knew it wouldn't! I can't read War and Peace! What about The Three Bears I say! Something short!'

But he spoke to an empty bed. The Queen was racing down the corridors to the banqueting hall where the meeting was nearly over. They had chosen three options and taken a vote.

The Prime Minister's wife was reading the results.

'In reverse order,' she announced importantly. 'Third, a swift sudden spanking, the Cook's idea. Tempting, I must admit, but with possibly appalling consequences! Second, boarding school in a foreign country. Expensive and undiplomatic! First, negotiate betrothal agreement with a view to future long term matrimonial disposal ...'

'The sooner the better,' interrupted the Cook excitedly, 'and you'll need to get the intended tied down legal and proper with no means of escape because if you ask me she gets Worse Every Day!'

'WHO gets worse every day?' demanded the Queen bouncing in.

'You're supposed to be in bed,' said the Prime Minister's wife. 'Still, I suppose it doesn't matter now. We've decided that it's time to begin the process of selection and engagement ...'

'Marry you off!' explained the Cook with satisfaction.

'Off what?' demanded the Queen.

'It is a figure of speech,' explained the Prime Minister's wife. 'But in due course, after a period of betrothal and always supposing a suitable party can be induced to agree, you will be expected to marry ...'

'Marry what?' asked the Queen suspiciously.

'Marry whom, you should say,' replied the

Prime Minister's wife. 'A Prince of course, responsible, reliable and rich. Perhaps from a Distant Land. Should you like that?'

'Well I shouldn't mind much,' said the Queen surprisingly. 'Especially if we can send the Ladies-in-Waiting to distant lands to look for him.'

'Certainly not, we will invite them here,' said the Prime Minister's wife much to the Queen's disappointment.

'They'll have to be Practically Perfect,' added the Queen, 'and with jet-black hair and very posh clothes and crowns like goodness knows what!'

'What about The Three Bears?' asked the Prime Minister, who was very much behind the times.

'They would do,' said the Queen graciously.

'Well, I don't think you should do it,' said Michael.

'You shut up!' said everyone except the Queen.

'Do what?' asked the Queen.

'Say you'll go and marry anyone,' said Michael.

'Don't let them make you!'

'I shan't if I don't want to,' said the Queen.

Several days later the Prime Minister's wife came
hurrying out to the Royal Stables to look for the
Queen.

'They've come then,' said Michael.

'Who?' asked the Queen.

'The practically perfect, jet-black haired,
responsible, reliable and rich Princes from distant
lands you said you would promise to marry,'
replied the Prime Minister's wife.

'Oh,' said the Queen. 'I'll go and have a look at
them then.'

They were all on the palace front steps, bowing
like mad to each other and dressed in their best
clothes and most beautiful crowns (as the
advertisement had advised). When the Queen
came up to them they pointed their bows at her.

'Very posh clothes,' remarked the Queen to

Michael, who had tagged along too, and they all
smirked.

'I have two questions to ask you,' said the
Queen importantly. 'Michael has written them

down for me. Give me the paper Michael.'

Michael passed the Queen a piece of paper and she read out, 'One. What would you do if you married me?'

'Govern the country,' they replied in chorus. 'To save you worrying!'

'Oh,' said the Queen. 'Well. Two. What are you hobbies and interests?'

'HuntinShootinFishin,' they answered altogether.

'HuntinShootinFishin What?' demanded the Queen.

'Anything. Animals. Birds. Fish,' replied the Princes.

'Donkeys?' asked the Queen.

'Donkeys,' agreed the Princes languidly. 'Could do.'

That was the end of them of course. They were packed off to their distant lands as fast as the Queen could summon the police.

'Very naughty!' said the Prime Minister's wife. 'Chasing them like that! I thought they were exactly what you wanted!'

'Too stuck up,' said the Queen. 'Horrible posh clothes and horrible posh crowns and horrible, horrible hobbies! Anyway, I like bright gold hair best! And I'm going back out to the stables to brush the Royal Donkey!'

Several weeks later the Prime Minister's wife came mincing across the stable yard.

'Come then have they?' asked Michael gloomily.

'What?' asked the Queen.

'The practically perfect, golden haired, responsible, reliable and rich Princes from distant lands you said you would promise to marry,' replied the Prime Minister's wife.

'Oh,' said the Queen. 'I'll come and have a look at them then.'

'I'll come too,' said Michael.

They were lying on the front lawn throwing daisies at each other. Warned by the advertisement, they wore the oldest rags available in their distant lands.

'Hiya!' they called to the Queen. 'Come on! Sit down! Have a daisy!'

'Awful clothes,' commented the Queen at which they all smirked, 'and they're MY daisies! Answer my questions! One. What would you do if you married me?'

'Govern your country,' they replied cheerfully, 'to save you from worrying.'

'Oh,' said the Queen. 'Well. Two, what are your hobbies and interests?'

These Princes had done their homework.

'Nursing and cosetting donkeys!' they announced as one.

'What, my Royal Donkey?' demanded the Queen.

'Your Royal Donkey,' agreed the Princes carelessly. 'Scrub it, hose it, scrape out its feet, the lot! You need never do another thing!'

Obviously that was the end of those Princes. They departed for their distant lands hotly pursued by the army.

'Very, very naughty!' said the Prime Minister's

wife. 'I thought they'd be just right!'

'Too rude and scruffy,' said the Queen airily.
'Very bad for the daisies and horrible, horrible
hobbies! Anyway, I think I only like fire-red hair!
And I'm going back to the stables to talk to the
Royal Donkey. Come on Michael!'

Several months later the Prime Minister's wife
came running across the lawn.

'Oh,' said Michael. 'Pity!'

'What?' asked the Queen.

'He's come,' said the Prime Minister's wife.
'There was only one practically perfect, fire-red
haired, responsible, reliable, rich Prince from a
distant land like you said you would promise to
marry and he's waiting in the banqueting hall.

'Oh,' said the Queen. 'I'll come and have a look
at him then. Are you coming Michael?'

'Might as well,' said Michael.

The Prince was staring out of the window,
talking to himself about the weather. He wore

very ordinary clothes and a sort of crownish hat
and he tried to shake hands with the Queen.

'What would you do if you married me?' asked
the Queen, yawning already.

'Govern your country to save you worrying,'
he replied.

'Oh,' said the Queen. 'Well. What are your hobbies and interests?'

'Haven't got any,' he replied very cunningly.

'Boring, boring, boring,' said the Queen as Michael showed him the door.

'Very, very, very naughty,' said the Prime Minister's wife. 'I thought he would be ideal! What do you want them to say?'

'I don't know,' said the Queen dismally.

'Something friendly,' suggested Michael.

'Yes,' said the Queen. 'Something friendly! What would you do Michael if you married me?'

'Me?' asked Michael. 'Nothing much. Just be here like I always am. Give you a hand with the Ladies-in-Waiting if you wanted. Nothing much.'

'Good,' said the Queen. 'I can govern my country perfectly well! I never worry! And what are your hobbies and interests?'

'You know what they are as well as I do!' replied Michael. 'They're just the things we do all day. But

I don't think you should do it!'

'Do what?'

'Promise to marry some practically perfect, responsible, reliable, rich Prince from a distant land,' said Michael.

'Who do you think I should marry then?' asked the Queen.

'Me,' said Michael.

'All right,' said the Queen.

Of course there was great opposition. To have the Queen betrothed to Michael would not solve any of the problems at the palace. They would not get rid of her at all. They pointed out that Michael was not a Prince, nor responsible, nor reliable, nor rich, nor did he come from a distant land. On the contrary, he lived in a room over the stables.

'And he has brown hair!' snapped the Prime Minister's wife.

'Who cares?' asked the Queen. 'I think he is

Practically Perfect!'

'Ridiculous!' grumbled the Prime Minister. 'This is Real Life, not a Fairy Tale!'

The Queen and Michael took absolutely no notice. They were betrothed at once and married

on the Queen's eighteenth birthday (with the gypsy girl as chief bridesmaid and the Royal Donkey carrying the train) and then they lived happily ever after, exactly like a fairy tale but with even more adventures.

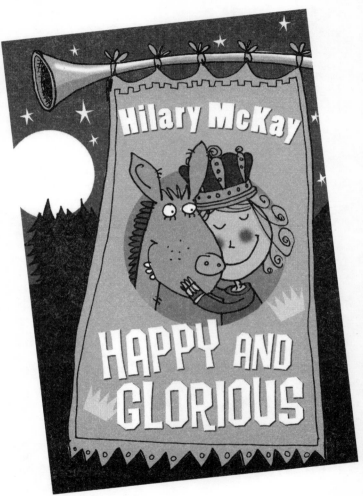

978 0 340 97023 2